BLOOD IN THE SAND

STACIE BARTOLOTTO
Photographed by: Dave Clearihue

BLOOD IN THE SAND

ReadersMagnet, LLC

Blood In The Sand
Copyright © 2021 by: Stacie Bartolotto

Published in the United States of America
ISBN Paperback: 978-1-955603-08-9
ISBN Hardback: 978-1-955603-09-6
ISBN eBook: 978-1-955603-07-2

All rights reserved. No part of this publication may be reproduced, stored in a retrieval system or transmitted in any way by any means, electronic, mechanical, photocopy, recording or otherwise without the prior permission of the author except as provided by USA copyright law.

ReadersMagnet, LLC
10620 Treena Street, Suite 230 | San Diego, California, 92131 USA
1.619.354.2643 | www.readersmagnet.com

Book design copyright © 2021 by: ReadersMagnet, LLC. All rights reserved.
Cover Design, Photograph by: Dave Clearihue
Interior design by: Renalie Malinao

Contents

▬ ▬ ▬ ▬ ▬ ▬ ▬ ▬ ▬ ▬ ▬

Dedication vii

Three Months Earlier. 1
On The Road 7
Cottonwood Visitors' Center. 11
Ryan's Ranch 14
Keys View 17
Adobe Campgrounds 19
Help!. 23
Stranded 26
Gas Station & Cafe. 28
Driving Home 29

Dedication

For Dave

I do appreciate you for always being there, Dave. I hope you will love the book. I will make it as an audiobook as well. Thank you for taking me to Joshua Tree National Park and to the desert. You got me liking the desert now. I will always treasure the moments when we would always go out there. We have accomplished this together because you were involved in the writing process by taking me to both places.

To my kids

Thank you for driving me crazy and keeping me on my toes at all times. You both are my life and I want to thank you as well because you have shown me that we can have fun and enjoy what we have accomplished together.

I love you all and I wouldn't have done this book without you by my side.

Three Months Earlier

▬ ▬ ▬ ▬ ▬ ▬ ▬ ▬ ▬ ▬ ▬ ▬

When Misty got home, she heard the answering machine beep for a little bit but she was tired from work. She had her purse and backpack on her so she put the bags down on the couch and walked over to the kitchen counter to see who called. Misty pushed the button. "Hey, Misty, its Hayley! Well, I wanted to talk to you about this weekend and see if you're free because Slim, Jayden, and I wanted to go to Joshua Tree National Park to have some fun and we want you with us. So are you in? If so, please give me a call back or stop by, okay. Talk to you later."

After Misty heard the message, she thought about it. She knew it was time for her to get out and have some fun with her friends and her younger sister. All she did each day was work.

The next day was Friday. As she went to work, Misty saw Ms. Grayson whom she had known for a long time. Vicky was slender with long black hair and brown eyes. Misty had gone into her office and asked Vicky if she could take the day off since she had been working like a dog.

"Come in, Misty, what could I do for you today?" Vicky asked.

"Well, I wanted to ask you if I can have a day off from work because this weekend I'm going to Joshua Tree National Park with some friends and my younger sister. Do you know, if there are any unsolved mysteries up there?" Misty asked, with excitement in her voice.

"That's fine, but there's a mystery that needs to be solved. There's a woman missing out near Joshua Tree National Park but I don't know if you can do it. If you can't, give Houston a call. You remember him, don't you? You went to school with him," Vicky said, with a smile.

"Oh wow, I will do what I can to solve the mystery. Oh yes, I do remember Houston. He was a long time friend of mine but we lost touch. Where could I reach him?"

"Well, you're going to be shocked to learn he works as a detective at Desert Springs Police Department close to here," Vicky said.

"I had been wanting to get in touch with him for a long time! Do you know his direct number so I can reach him?" Misty wondered.

"Yeah, I got it. You can write down the number or put it in your phone so you won't lose it," Vicky said, giggling.

"Alrighty, I got it in my contacts and I do appreciate your help and I will touch base with you as soon as I get there. Thank you." Misty returned a smile and walked out of the office.

"You're welcome." Vicky smiled back.

Misty gathered all the information from her desk regarding the missing woman and walked towards the door as she waved at Vicky. She got into her truck and drove off to go see her friend, Hayley, and tell her the good news.

As Misty drove off, she looked over some of the old buildings and some houses, old and new. She finally arrived at Hayley's house. Misty honked the horn. Hayley walked fast to Misty's truck. They gave each other a hug.

"Well, look who decided to come over. So did you get my message about going to Joshua Tree National Park?" Hayley asked, wondering.

"Of course I did, Hayley. I would love to go so I got the rest of the day off from work. Plus there's a story about a missing woman that I have to check out but we will have fun, trust me. So where's Slim and Jayden?" Misty said.

"Oh they're here, just waiting for you to come over or call but since you're here, I can call them out," Hayley said.

"Okay, I'll be in the truck when you go get the girls," Misty said.

Hayley walked towards the door and called Slim and Jayden out so they can go. It was about 2pm in the afternoon. Misty had Jayden sit up front with her and Slim in the backseat of truck.

As she was driving, she noticed the mountains were blood orange and there were trees and cactus all around. Misty was silent. She had something on her mind. There were few cars on the highway. Misty saw a sign states highway 62 on the right hand side. Hayley asks:

"So what's this story you suppose to write about?" Hayley said.

"All I know is, there's a missing woman at Joshua Tree National Park and the police are looking for this woman. I guess she's been missing since Thursday," Misty said.

"Now I'm wondering who would do such a thing and who knows if she's hurt as well?" Slim said.

"Yeah, I'm with Slim right there too, Misty. Why would anyone want to hurt the woman? She doesn't deserve that," Jayden said.

"I don't know ladies, but all I do know, if something happens to my sister, the man will pay for it," Misty said in a stern voice.

They made it to Ryan's Ranch at around 4:30pm in the evening. Hayley, Slim, and Jayden got out of the truck to head for the trail. Misty was at the truck to get the flashlight.

"Hey Misty, we're going to head for Ryan's Ranch before it gets dark, okay?" Hayley said.

"Be careful and call me if there's any trouble," Misty said, concerned.

They went on the trail and Misty could hear them giggling all the way to the adobe home. *It's beautiful here and the park has red rocks when the sun hits on them. Well, I found my flashlight so now I can go on the trail and catch up with them, Misty thought.* As she was walking on the trail, she noticed shoe prints that looked like hiking or work boots. *So there were a lot of Joshua trees around.* She took pictures of the plants.

As Misty looked around, she heard her friends and her sister yelling but then they stopped. Misty went towards the adobe home. She sees her sister, Jayden, lying there with blood and she went to her but she was dead before Misty got to her and her friends. Tears coming down her cheeks, Misty tried to run to her truck for safety but the man was standing by the trail as she turned around to look. Finally, she got to her truck and as she closed the door, the man held it and told her, *"You better watch yourself!"* And he let go of the door. It was 8pm. As she drove off, she called Houston but couldn't get a signal. Its hard to get a decent signal at Joshua Tree National Park.

Misty drove out of the park and called Houston:

"Hey, Houston, it's Misty, I need your help, My friends and my sister were here at Joshua Tree National Park to have fun and I was going to find out what happened to the missing woman but never got the chance," Misty said, crying.

"Oh Misty, I will be right out to you as soon as I can. Where can I meet you?" Houston said, frantically.

"Well, I'm at the west entrance of Joshua Tree National Park so I'll be here and wait for you. I have a black Silverado truck; you should see it when you come out here," Misty said.

"Okay, see you then."

As Misty was waiting for Houston to get there, she had to use the restroom so she hurriedly went and got back to her truck and sat there.

Misty was happy to see sirens about a mile away. Houston looked horrified when he saw her.

"Misty, I will be back, I promise, okay?" Houston said.

"All right then. See you when you get back here and please be careful," Misty said.

As Misty was waiting, Houston and his partner went up to Ryan's Ranch to look for clues. Sure enough, they found blood splatter on the walls inside the adobe home but no bodies and no sign of the man who killed Misty's friends and her sister.

"She's going to be really upset when she finds out that they aren't here," Houston said, shaking his head.

"Man, this isn't good, that's for sure. Well, we can come back here tomorrow morning and see what we can find because it's already dark out here and we can't see anything," Parker said.

"First thing, I'm going to do is get out here as soon as possible because the weather out here will be hot so we have to be here just before the sun comes up," Houston said.

As they were walking on the trail, they spotted some blood drops heading towards the highway so that gave Houston a clue that the man got out.

They drove back to where Misty was. He knows she would be really upset but he had to tell her.

Misty was desperate and she wanted to know what was happening. She saw a pair of headlights coming down the highway and it was Houston and his partner.

Houston got out of his car. He couldn't look at Misty but he started by saying,

"We found some blood splatters on the wall of the adobe home but we couldn't find the bodies anywhere," Houston said, feeling upset.

"Oh my gosh! Really? How could I be that stupid to let them go?! We were having so much fun that I didn't think about them getting killed. So are you going to come out here again tomorrow?" Misty said.

"Yes, I'm coming out but I want you to go home and get some rest, okay? I will let you know what I find out," Houston said.

Misty jumped into the truck and started driving out of the park but she sensed something wasn't right but there was nothing she could do but get her revenge against the man who did this to her friends and her sister.

On The Road

━ ━ ━ ━ ━ ━ ━ ━ ━ ━ ━ ━

Misty had just gotten up when she heard a thunk, as if someone had thrown a rock at her door. She rushed to the door and opened it but she didn't see anyone. Then she noticed there was a note on her front door. Chills ran down her spine as she picked it up. The note stated: *you better watch yourself.*

As she stood there, she thought back on what had happened to her friends and her younger sister.

Back inside, she sat down to think about how she was going to get this man. As Misty peered out the window, there was a tree in front with birds chirping and there was a nest where the birds had their young. There was something else on the note but she couldn't make it out. Getting a pencil from her desk in the living room, Misty drew a line lightly back and forth with the pencil, revealing the imprint of the letter H. *So what does that mean?*

She hurriedly packed her duffel bag and her laptop, deciding she could do her work while she was up there at Twenty-Nine Palms near the National Park. The keys to her truck were on the counter in her kitchen so she grabbed them and headed out the door, locking it behind her.

She started her truck and drove out towards the highway. Now she had a gut feeling that the man was going to be there but she wasn't sure because of what took place there. The palms of her hands were sweating even though she had the air conditioner on. She was very nervous. She saw the sign that says Twenty-Nine Palms the next three miles. The road was a highway and it had always been dangerous because too many drunk drivers drove on this road. She wrote a story about it in the newspaper and she would get comments from people who read her article.

As she was driving, she saw a rabbit run across the street in a distance and after that she saw two quails crossing the street a little while later. She could see the mountains and the desert plants around, just like what she remembered. As she drove, she saw the sign: Twenty-Nine Palms city limits so she was happy that she made it there.

It was about 12pm. There was a motel close to Park Boulevard, so Misty went there to check in. She parked in the lot, got out to head for the lobby. As she stepped in, she saw a desk and chairs in the lobby. There was a man behind the desk and his name was Landon Austin. Misty went up to the desk.

"Hi there, I would like to get a room."

"Okay, before I can check you in, may I have your name first so I can see if you reserved a room?" Landon said.

"My name is Misty Rayborn," Misty told him.

"Well, I didn't find you in the computer but I can have a room for you as soon as possible if you want to wait for about 15 minutes or so," Landon asked.

"Sure, I could wait here until the maids are done with the room," Misty said politely.

"All right, miss, I will book you in and give you the card as soon as they get done."

"That would be good, thank you."

As Misty got out her bank card out, she handed it to him and Landon got it so he can swipe it and had Misty sign the receipt. Landon gave her the receipt for her records so she got the card back and put it in her laptop bag. She sat in the chair to read a magazine when she noticed a black Thunderbird parked across the street. She stood up as she peered out the window and she was surprised it wasn't the same car she remembered. Misty's heart skipped a beat and it scared her.

As she was going to sit back down, Landon called her over to the desk and told her,

"Here's the card key to the door. If for any reason you have trouble getting into your room, give me a call and I can help you right away."

"Oh, thank you so much! I will keep that in mind."

As she was walking towards the door, she waved at Landon as she was leaving. Misty got into her truck, drove over to her room, and parked right in front of the building, so she could keep an eye out on her truck. It was about 2:30pm. Misty got her duffel bag and her laptop from the truck and she opened the door, went into the room and put her stuff on the bed. Now since she was there, she wanted to go to Cottonwood Visitor's Center so as she unpacked her stuff, she walked out of her room with her purse and the keys to head to Joshua Tree National Park.

Misty was nervous as she headed to the visitor's center because she didn't know what to expect when she got there. She turned right on Park Boulevard. As she drove, she could feel her stomach tightening, but she must get the story of what happened to the woman who went missing a week ago. So, she drove towards the visitors' center after paying a fee.

Cottonwood Visitors' Center

▬ ▬ ▬ ▬ ▬ ▬ ▬ ▬ ▬ ▬ ▬ ▬ ▬

As she was driving, she saw fewer people at the National Park which was great because she'd be able to do her research on what happened. She stopped at the Cholla Garden and sat there for a moment to get her thoughts together, then she got out of the truck and took some pictures of the garden. She walked towards the trail when she saw quails going by and few small squirrels scattered, admiring the sparrows as she went.

It was 3:30pm when she got into her truck and started driving.

She drove to the visitors' center, close to the restrooms.

They had a bulletin board with information from safety to wildlife in the park. Misty went into the visitors' center and asked for Nicky Westgate.

"Ah, hi, I'm here to see Nicky Westgate. Is he available?" Misty asked.

"Okay, just wait here and I'll get him for you," the girl said, looking for Nicky.

Misty decided to walk around and saw they had stuffed animals for the kids and bird books on how to spot them out in the field like in the desert. Also, they had tee shirts and sweaters with designs on them.

"Hi there, you were looking for me, Ms. Rayborn?" Nicky asked, with a smile.

"Yes, I'm from the Palm Tree Newspaper and I want to ask you a few questions. Do you know what happened to the woman who went missing on Thursday of last week? Secondly, do you know who took her?" Misty said, having a pen and paper ready.

"Well, when I heard about what happened to the woman, I got dressed and got out here to see if I can locate her but I couldn't. I saw shoeprints near Ryan's Ranch as I was leaving," Nicky said, feeling bad.

"Hopefully we can find her, especially if you found shoeprints," Misty said, biting her nails.

"I just want to find this woman but I get the feeling that I won't be able to," Nicky said, worried.

"Hang in there. I will be here with you till you find her. We could start at Adobe Campgrounds," Misty said.

"All right, we will go but first I have to do some paperwork. I could meet you at Adobe Campgrounds in about an hour," Nicky answered.

"Great, I'll meet you there soon then," Misty said.

As Misty gathered her stuff, she waved at Nicky as she walked out. She put her stuff in the truck and went to the water fountain to drink but it wasn't working so she got a water bottle from the vending machine. As she walked towards her truck, she noticed a sticky note on her windshield, it stated: *Go home or else!* She grabbed the note and threw it on the ground. *I'm not going anywhere, she thought.* Misty got into the truck and started driving towards Ryan's Ranch.

Ryan's Ranch

■ ■ ■ ■ ■ ■ ■ ■ ■ ■ ■ ■

As she drove, she saw a jackrabbit running through the bushes and out of sight. Misty was heading for Ryan's Ranch when she spotted a dark patch in the distance. A mine? She was sure of it.

Misty saw people with their families, and Misty saw movement on the mountain and with the window cracked open, she could smell the aroma of hamburgers and hot dogs barbecuing on a grill, reminding her that she hadn't eaten since early morning. But she had to get to the ranch to investigate the murders of her sister and her friends.

When she got to Ryan's Ranch, she saw a black car in the parking lot, so she got out slowly and walked over to the car, but no one was in it. She looked over where the adobe home was, and she saw a man standing inside the home near where the window used to be. She jumped back into her truck because she didn't know who it was. The man, slender, 6'0 feet tall, clean-cut, and good-looking, started to walk back to his car. She got out and started to walk on the trail when the man drove off.

She had that eerie feeling about the man and her heart was racing when he walked to his car and left. She got on the trail around 3:30pm, so she had to work as the sun was beating on her skin and it was humid out, so she wore shorts and a tank top. She wore comfortable shoes to walk.

Misty walked towards the adobe home when she came across a Heart Locket lying on the ground. *It looks like the Heart Locket Jayden had when I last saw her*, Misty thought. She picked it up and put it in her bag, so she looked around to find more clues, but she found none. So as she walked back to her truck, she saw some writing on the rock, and it said: *I'm watching you*. When she read that, she began to keep a look out on the man, and it terrified her to the core. She would get her revenge on him after what he had done.

She looked closely at the ground because she knew her friends would have left something behind but that if he took it, she wouldn't find it. She got on the trail and started to walk towards the truck. When she got to her truck, Misty began to walk around the vehicle to make sure the man didn't touch it. She grabbed her keys to get into her truck when she saw Nicky arrived there.

Misty was standing by the bulletin board when she saw Nicky, and so Misty waved and yelled out, "I found a Heart Locket that belong to my sister Jayden."

"So they were murdered here then?" Nicky asked.

"Yes, the last time I had seen them, they were walking on the path going towards Ryan's Ranch that night," Misty said, almost in tears.

"Oh, I'm sorry about your friends and your sister. I'm sure we will find out who did this to them," Nicky said, comforting Misty.

"Well, I'm going to find out because nobody kills my sister and gets away with it!" Misty said.

"Okay, I'm always at the Visitors' Center from 7:30am to 6:30pm if you need me for anything."

"Thank you so much! I will be in touch," Misty said, getting into her truck.

She started the truck and drove off. She looked in the distance to see if anyone was at the adobe home but there wasn't anybody. So she drove towards the west entrance of the park to get to her motel room that was located at the edge of the park. When she finally reached her motel room, she got out to put the alarm on and that's when she spotted the man but he was in the car close to the entrance and he bolted out of there. As she stood there watching, she felt this eeriness around him like he was a serial killer. Misty rushed inside and locked the door behind her.

Keys View

▬ ▬ ▬ ▬ ▬ ▬ ▬ ▬ ▬ ▬ ▬

The next morning, Misty got up to get dressed, so she could get the day rolling. As she came out of the bathroom, she heard a car screeching on the asphalt. She looked out of the window and there he was, standing by the end of the road. *What does he want from me?*

She closed the curtain and got ready to head out when she heard the car again. *So he's gone for now.* She shut the door and locked it behind her, got into her truck, and headed for Keys View.

As she drove, she noticed something odd about the Locket she picked up from Ryan's Ranch. Misty got to Keys View. She parked and sat in the truck then noticed that it was Jayden's heart locket that mom gave her on her 21st birthday. Suddenly, Misty felt something sticky, so she turned it around and it had blood on the heart. While she was sitting in the truck, tears rolled down her cheeks because her sister meant so much to her.

As Misty sat there, she saw Nicky was there waiting for her and he was trying to guide people down toward the parking lot. Misty noticed a small bag by the bench, so she rushed over there to pick it up. She walked up to the walkway and saw Nicky looking down on the city. She walked up to him.

"Hey, Nicky, I wanted to tell you, I'm thankful you are here to help me," Misty said.

"No problem, Misty, I'm glad to help you and I want to catch this guy too," Nicky said.

"Alright then, we should start here and if we can't find anything, then we can go back to Ryan's Ranch. That's where I found my sister's locket. Our mom got it for her when she turned 21," Misty said, blinking back tears.

"Okay, I will keep my eyes open for her belongings then," Nicky said, putting his hand on her shoulder.

"Well, I'm going to see if I can find any clues but if not, I'm going back to Ryan's Ranch and see if I can find any of my sister's things," Misty said, wiping her tears away.

So Misty started looking for things that would give her a clue to what happened. Presently, she had two stories to write. One was about a teenager and the other one was about her sister and their friends.

When she got up to the top of the stairs, she sat there, looked out at the city below, and thought about her friends and Jayden. *I really miss them a lot*, she thought.

Misty walked to the parking lot and that's when she saw a note on her windshield it read: *You better stop or else!* Someone was trying to scare her but she wasn't going to budge until she found the man who murdered her sister and her friends.

She got into her truck and drove towards Ryan's Ranch. She was halfway down the hill when she saw a black car coming up so fast. She pulled into the turnout as the car went by. She breathed out slowly. Then she got back on the highway to head for the Ranch.

Adobe Campgrounds

▬ ▬ ▬ ▬ ▬ ▬ ▬ ▬ ▬ ▬ ▬ ▬ ▬

Misty was heading towards Ryan's Ranch, when she saw something at the campgrounds, so she drove straight there.

When she pulled into the parking lot, she scanned around to see if she could find anything she recognized. She got out and started to walk towards the restrooms. Misty noticed there was a little blood drip in the sink, so she went to her truck and got a swab, so she can take it to Houston. She hoped it would be a match but she wouldn't be sure until she took it to him. She called Nicky at 12:30pm.

"This is Nicky, how can I help you today?" Nicky said.

"Hi there, it's Misty. I wanted to know if you wouldn't mind meeting me out here at the Adobe campgrounds," Misty said, wondering if he would meet her.

"Hey, Misty. Sure, I can help you but let me finish my paperwork first and I will head out there," Nicky said, wanting to help Misty.

"Okay, I will be walking around but I won't walk too far from my truck so I will be here when you get here," Misty said, happy.

"Alright, see you then, bye," Nicky said.

As she walked towards the trail, she saw the heavy shoe prints on the dirt. Misty decided to take a picture. *Maybe that's the killer's shoes.* So, she proceeded but the sign said Ryan's Ranch Trail. So she walked until she got to the rocks. That was when she noticed there was a key to something. Misty picked it up and put it into her pocket. She started to walk back and she saw the mountains around her and breathed in fresh air. It was a little windy but warm to the touch. She was almost to her truck when she noticed tire tracks on the asphalt. She took a picture of it with her phone. Since she had her laptop at the motel, she could download it and look at the pictures when she drove back.

Misty walked towards her truck when she spotted Nicky in his car. Now she could tell him what she found in the restroom. As Misty walked over to him, he was getting out of his car.

"So what did you find here?" Nicky said, wondering what it was.

"Well, I found a blood drip in the restroom and I took a swab and saved it, so I can take it to Houston," Misty said, hoping it would be the killer's blood.

"It won't be as easy to find anything because this is a big National Park," Nicky said.

"Okay, I realize it's a big National Park but I've got to try and get as much as evidence I could, so I can send it to Houston."

"That would be great, so let's find some clues then," Nicky said as he walked away.

Misty walked towards the rocks, when she saw someone standing there with binoculars looking at what she was doing. So, Misty turned back and walked to the campgrounds. She already knew she was being watched, especially when she received a note on her door several days ago on Friday. When she was walking back, she looked behind her to see if the man was up on the rocks but he was gone. Misty walked back towards her truck, when Nicky walked up to her.

"So, what did you find on the trail?" Nicky said.

"Well, I was walking towards the rocks when I saw someone looking at me and he had something on him like a bowie knife," Misty said, worried.

"Stay off of the trails at night because there are too many things that can happen! Especially at night," Nicky said, watching out for her safety.

"I know but we can go out to Ryan's Ranch soon and see what we can find there," Misty said, getting anxious about finding Jayden's and her friends' killer.

"Sure, we can head out there in the morning and I will see you then," Nicky said, heading to his car.

"Alright then, I will get out here sometime. See you then," Misty said, waving at Nicky as he was leaving.

Misty got into her truck to grab her jacket and she started to head towards Ryan's Ranch. She desperately wanted to find out who had done this to her friends and her sister. As she stopped at the entrance of the trail, she looked in the distance and started thinking about what happened. The temperature was warm in the afternoon but in the evening, it was cooler.

It was 3pm when she left Ryan's Ranch Trail. She drove towards the south entrance of the National Park. She had about a half tank of gas when she realized she needed to get more. Misty knew she was traveling alone and there was no cell service to call for help. Misty hoped she'd make it to the south entrance of the park. She knew it was a long drive from the campgrounds. As she drove, she thought about the case she was covering and how that had been affecting her emotionally. She had fought back tears from falling but then she noticed a car had been following her since she left the ranch.

Help!

━ ━ ━ ━ ━ ━ ━ ━ ━ ━ ━ ━ ━

It was about 4pm when Misty got into her truck and drove towards the visitors' center, which can be seen from a distance. She thought about Jayden and her friends and how she missed them so much! The guy who killed them wouldn't get away with it. She was driving on Park Boulevard when she saw a car coming up fast but she couldn't see who was in it. She pulled into the turnouts, so the guy could pass her. Misty continued and drove to Pinto Basin Road. It was then Misty knew who the killer was but she was not sure. She had the file in her suitcase, so she stopped at Belle Campgrounds, so she could get the information. *It should tell me who killed Jayden and her friends.* Misty got out and grabbed the suitcase to open it. She put the file on the console. She jumped back into the truck and scanned through the documents. The name was smeared but it did have a letter D.

Misty started driving when she saw something shiny up the road. It was a flashlight, so she got closer to it and it was the young woman who went missing for a week. The temperature was cooler than expected but the woman needed help, so Misty drove to the visitors' center to get help for the woman.

"So, what happened, why are you out here by yourself?" Misty wondered.

"Well, this guy picked me up from Amboy and I needed a ride home but he didn't take me home and he wanted to harm me!" the woman said, shivering.

"Why would he want to harm you?" Misty said, chills down her spine.

"He said I look like someone he knew in high school but he didn't tell me the woman's name because he figured I would talk about it," the woman said.

"Oh my gosh, that's me! I was in high school when I got attacked but I didn't know the boy's name," Misty said.

"That's why he grabbed me and kept me where no one would ever see me out here," the woman said.

"Okay, I'm going to take you to the visitors' center. There's a guy who works there named Nicky and he could help you get home as soon as possible," Misty said.

It was 4:30pm when she picked up the woman who was barely wearing anything. The woman had a tee-shirt and shorts with tennis shoes. As Misty drove, she thought about what the woman was talking about. *So it was someone from my past.* It was a few years ago when Misty graduated from high school. She was trying to jar her memory who the boy was back then. But she had to forget about it because she had to focus on what she was doing.

Misty and the woman arrived at the visitors' center and got out of the truck. She noticed Nicky was still there, so she walked up to him and told him,

"Here's the woman I was looking for and she's safe now."

"Oh, I was wondering what happened to her," Nicky said with a sigh of relief.

"The guy kidnapped her and kept her for a week," Misty said.

Nicky called her parents and told them what happened. They were on their way to pick her up. So Misty stayed there to be with her. It was then she saw the guy in the car, driving by, pointing at her with an evil smile on his face. Misty tried to look at his face but he turned away.

"Nicky, I need to go home and get some sleep and I will be back out here soon. If you hear anything, please let me know and I will head back here again," Misty said, waving at him.

"Keep safe and I will let you know if I find anything," Nicky yelled, waving back.

Misty walked to her truck and drove towards the south entrance. She was very concerned about the woman being out here, knowing the temperatures were a little cooler than normal. It got pitch-black and scary out here in the desert. Misty had her Bowie knife for protection because she knew there were many dangers. So many things were going through Misty's mind -- she wondered who it could be and why. She shrugged it off and she was almost to the entrance.

Stranded

As Misty was about to turn, she realized she would be out of gas. So she drove straight to the gas station. It was bothering her since she picked up that woman. Since she was stranded, she had to get help to get her truck towed. Misty parked at the side of the freeway entrance to wait. She called the tow company and they wouldn't be out here for 2 hours. She looked at the file that Vicky gave her and looked through it but that letter D had stuck with her ever since she left Ryan's Ranch. All this just didn't make sense to her. So she left a message for Houston.

Houston, I need to talk to you because I found the woman at the National Park and she said the guy who grabbed her went to school with me. So it has to be someone I didn't associate with when I was in high school. As of right now, I'm stranded out here by the south entrance of Joshua Tree National Park. Please call me back when you get this message.

An hour went by and nothing yet. So she put some music on to keep her calm.

When she looked up, there were lights coming towards her. She was thankful that the man hooked up her truck, they got in, and headed to the gas station. Once they got there, Misty got out and the man put the truck beside the pumps, so she could get gas. Misty tells the man,

"I do appreciate you coming out to get me," Misty said, smiling at him.

"You're more than welcome, miss. I hope you get home safe now," the driver said, waving at her as he drove on to the street.

As he left, she waved at him. She could relax now.

Gas Station & Cafe

Misty got her bag out and grabbed her wallet, so she could get her card out. She was finally able to get gas and since she was waiting for the gas to be done, she kept an eye out for any movement. When the pump had finished, she put the pump back and got the cap on her tank.

She wanted something to drink, so she went into the store. That's when she called Houston to tell him she was safe. She got a water bottle and paid for it.

When she looked at the clock, it was 8:30pm. She parked her truck so she could get something to eat and look over the file once more. As she was looking through the file, she saw some notes on it that she didn't notice before. It had a photo of the woman but not the killer. *So why did the woman bring a friend with her?* She felt chills going down on her spine. This was a day Misty wouldn't forget. Misty started listening to a song that the cafe was playing. It was from a Canadian band. The song was Time Stands Still. As she was listening to it, she thought about her high school years and how the years had gone by too fast for her. She finished her meal and headed out.

As Misty was putting her file away, she closed her door.

Driving Home

▬ ▬ ▬ ▬ ▬ ▬ ▬ ▬ ▬ ▬ ▬ ▬ ▬

Misty had gotten into her truck when she saw the car, so she drove out of there and found the freeway onramp. It was a trying day and hopefully, she would find out who the killer was. All these feelings were coming up inside her and she could feel herself getting angry because of what the woman was saying. She didn't expect it but the one thing that got to Misty was her friends, Hayley and Slim. They were her two best friends and the killer had to choose them. Misty was really upset about the fact that the guy killed her sister and she got her Heart Locket. *Coming out here took a lot of me, she thought.* It was a time she didn't want to think about it because she could remember that night like yesterday.

She saw in the rearview mirror that she was being followed again. *Why can't this guy go away? What does he want from me?* She weaved in and out of traffic so he couldn't follow her home. She wanted to be left alone but this guy was so determined to keep her reminded of what happened at Ryan's Ranch.

She got on the highway because it was quicker. Misty thought she would lose him but he was coming up fast, so she stepped on the gas and drove a little faster. She was determined to put the guy behind bars for what he did. She was getting close to home now.

As she turned the corner, she noticed there were no lights in her house, so that really unnerved her and she didn't see a car in sight. So she parked in her driveway and got her bags and suitcase from the truck and went inside and she saw the answering machine was beeping.

Hi, Misty, I will come for you when you least expect it.